D0819984

COPY 1 8

| E | $11.89 |
| KRA | Krauss, Ruth |
| | The happy day |

| 149 | 23 |
| 103 | 33 |
| 14 | 35 |
| 19 | 38 |
| 1 | 132 |
| 8 | 139 |
| 12 | 150 |
| 16 | 160 |
| 22 | |

MONTEREY COUNTY
SALINAS
CALIFORNIA
LIBRARY

WITHDRAWN

T2-BTB-944

# OTHER BOOKS BY RUTH KRAUSS

# THE
# HAPPY DAY

MONTEREY COUNTY LIBRARY SALINAS CALIFORNIA WITHDRAWN

By
## RUTH KRAUSS
*Pictures by*
## MARC SIMONT

Harper & Row, Publishers
New York and Evanston

Hand set in Weiss Antiqua type by T. E. Mergendahl Jr.
at The Golden Hind Press in Madison, N. J.

Copyright, 1949, as to text, by Ruth Krauss. Copyright, 1949, as to pictures, by Marc Simont.
Printed in the United States of America. All rights in this book are reserved. No part of the book
may be reproduced in any manner whatsoever without written permission except in the case of brief
quotations embodied in critical articles and reviews. For information address
Harper & Row, Publishers, Incorporated,
10 East 53rd Street, New York, N.Y. 10022

# THE
# HAPPY DAY

Snow is falling.

The field mice are sleeping,

the bears are sleeping,

the little snails sleep in their shells;

and the squirrels sleep in the trees,

the ground hogs sleep in the ground.

Now, they open their eyes. They sniff.

The field mice sniff,

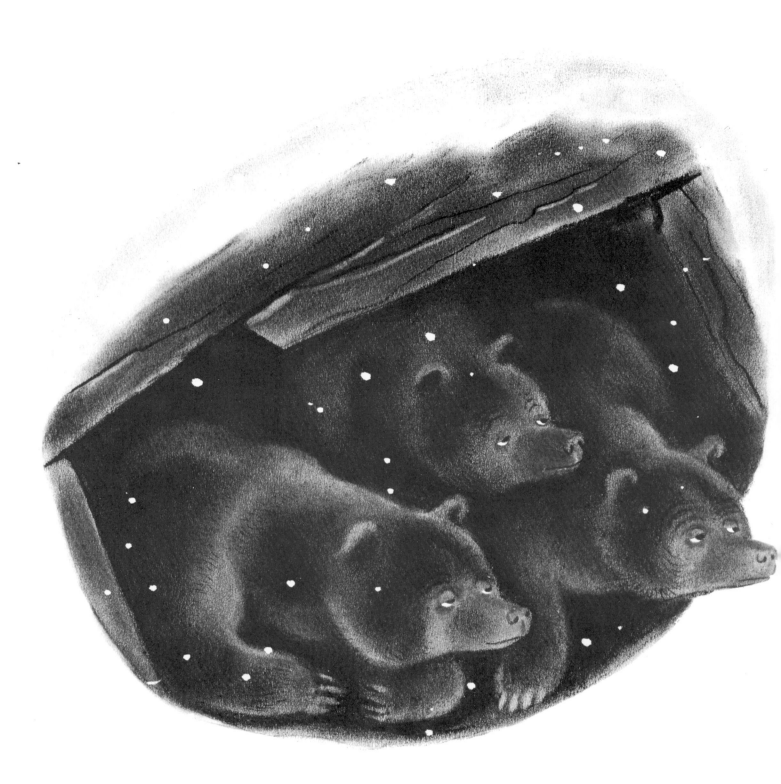

the bears sniff,

the little snails sniff in their shells;

and the squirrels sniff in the trees,

the ground hogs sniff in the ground.

They sniff.  They run.

The field mice run,

the bears run,

the little snails run with their shells,

and the squirrels run out of the trees,

the ground hogs run out of the ground.

They sniff. They run.

They run. They sniff.

They sniff. They run. They stop.

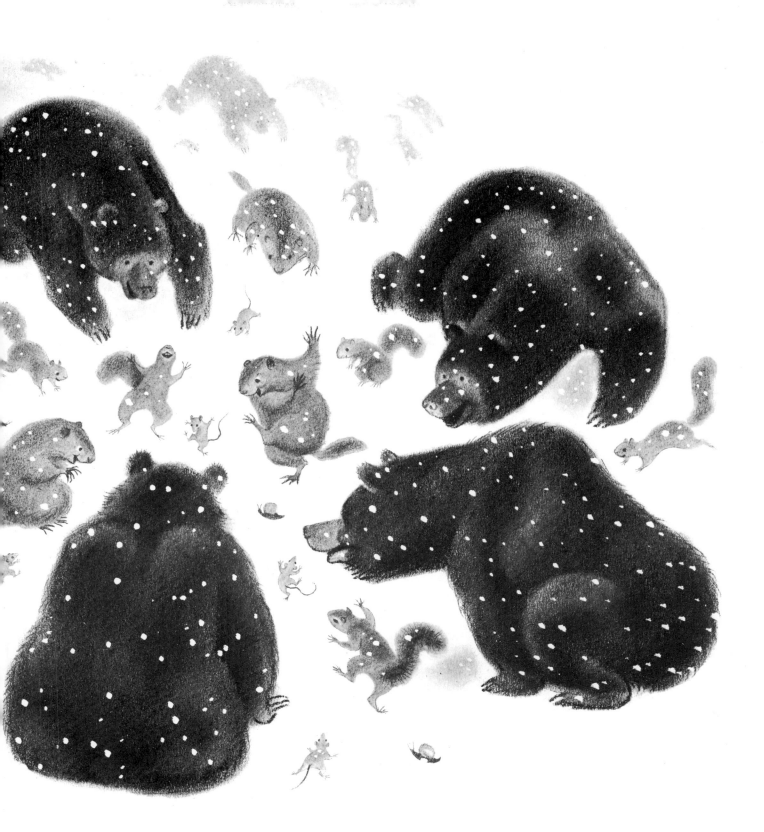

They stop.  They laugh.
They laugh.  They dance.

They cry, "Oh!
A flower is growing in the snow."